THE COVEN

AN EROTIC FAIRYTALE

VICTORIA RUSH

VOLUME 7

CLOVER'S FANTASY ADVENTURES -
BOOK 7

COPYRIGHT

ALSO BY VICTORIA RUSH

Adult Fairytales:

The Enchanted Forest: An Erotic Fairytale

The Land of Giants: An Erotic Fairytale

The Dragon's Lair: An Erotic Fairytale

Witch's Brew: An Erotic Fairytale

The Mage's Spell: An Erotic Fairytale

The Mermaid Lagoon: An Erotic Fairytale

The Coven: An Erotic Fairytale

Rapunzel: An Erotic Fairytale

The Seven Dwarfs: An Erotic Fairytale

The Land of Mutants: An Erotic Fairytale

The Erotic Temple: A Sexy Fairytale (Coming Soon)

Erotica Themed Bundles:

Voyeur: Lesbian Erotica Bundle

Public Affairs: A Lesbian Anthology

Futa Fantasies: The Ladyboy Collection

Threesomes: The Lesbian Collection

Threesomes - Volume 2: The Lesbian Collection

First Time: A Lesbian Anthology

Hedonism: An Erotic Anthology

Switch Hitters: Bisexual Erotica

Taboo Erotica: The Lesbian Series

BDSM: The Lesbian Collection

Party Games: The Erotic Collection

Party Games 2: The Erotic Collection

All Girl 1: Lesbian Erotica Bundle

All Girl 2: Lesbian Erotica Bundle

All Girl 3: Lesbian Erotica Bundle

All Girl 4: Lesbian Erotica Bundle

Erotic Fairytale Bundles:

Clover's Fantasy Adventures: Books 1 - 5

Clover's Fantasy Adventures: Books 6 - 10

Erotic Fantasy:

Pirate's Bounty: A Time Travel Adventure

Wild West: A Time Travel Adventure

Private Riley: A Time Travel Adventure

Cleopatra's Secret: A Time Travel Adventure

Bounty Hunter 2125: A Time Travel Adventure

Ninja Assassin: A Time Travel Adventure

The 300: A Time Travel Adventure

Arabian Nights: An Erotic Fairytale (coming soon...)

Steamy Time Travel Bundles:

Riley's Time Travel Adventures: Books 1 - 5

Lesbian Erotica:

The Dinner Party: Lesbian Voyeur Erotica

The Darkroom: Bisexual Voyeur Erotica

Naked Yoga: Lesbian Transgender Erotica

Nude Cruise: Bisexual Voyeur Erotica

Rush Hour: Taboo Public Sex

The Girl Next Door: First Time Lesbian Erotic Romance

Girls' Camp: Lesbian Group Sex

Wet Dream: Ladyboy Fantasy Erotica

The Convent: Taboo Sex with a Nun

Sex Robot: A Dream Sex Machine

The Personal Trainer: Getting Pumped at the Gym

The Dominatrix: BDSM Lesbian Domination

Webcam Chat: Lesbian Online Sex

Paint Me: A Kinky Bodypainting Workshop

The Toy Party: Girls Sharing Sex Toys

Riley's Time Travel Adventures: Books 1 - 5

Lesbian Erotica:

The Dinner Party: Lesbian Voyeur Erotica

The Darkroom: Bisexual Voyeur Erotica

Naked Yoga: Lesbian Transgender Erotica

Nude Cruise: Bisexual Voyeur Erotica

Rush Hour: Taboo Public Sex

The Girl Next Door: First Time Lesbian Erotic Romance

Girls' Camp: Lesbian Group Sex

Wet Dream: Ladyboy Fantasy Erotica

The Convent: Taboo Sex with a Nun

Sex Robot: A Dream Sex Machine

The Personal Trainer: Getting Pumped at the Gym

The Dominatrix: BDSM Lesbian Domination

Webcam Chat: Lesbian Online Sex

Paint Me: A Kinky Bodypainting Workshop

The Toy Party: Girls Sharing Sex Toys

The Costume Party: Strapping One On

Swedish Sauna: Lesbian Group Sex

The Therapist: Taboo Lesbian Erotica

Elevator Shaft: Bisexual Threesomes Erotica

Ladyboy: Lesbian Transgender Erotica

Peep Show: Lesbian Voyeur Erotica

The Dare: Public Sex Erotica

Maid Service: Lesbian Threesomes Erotica

The Hitchhiker: First Time Lesbian Erotica

The Housesitter: Spycam Lesbian Erotica

The Spa: Lesbian Group Orgy

Parlor Games: Blindfold Sex Party

The Exchange Student: First Time Lesbian Erotica

The Hostel: Bisexual Group Erotica

The Harem: Lesbian Erotic Romance

The Orient Express: Lesbian Voyeur Erotica

The First Lady: A Forbidden Lesbian Erotic Romance

The Slave: Lesbian BDSM Erotica

The Masseuse: Lesbian Sensuous Erotica

Too Close for Comfort: Lesbian Forbidden Erotica

Naked Twister: A Wild Party Game

Lexi: The Sex App (Lesbian Fantasy Erotica)

Call Girl: Lesbian Bisexual Threesomes Erotica

Circle Jill: Lesbian Masturbation Workshop

The Viewing Room: Masturbation Voyeur Erotica

Spin the Bottle: A Kinky Party Game

The Hair Salon: Lesbian Voyeur Erotica

Tribadism 1: Girls Only Sex Workshop

Tribadism 2: The Art of Scissoring

Tribadism 3: Threeway Hookups

The Kiss: A Game of Oral Sex

Pledge Week: Sorority Sisters

Carny Games 1: A Wild Sex Party

Carny Games 2: A Kinky Sex Party

Carny Games 3: An Erotic Sex Party

Dreamscape: An Artificial Reality Game

Glory Hole: Guess Who's On the Other Side

Joy Ride: A Late Night Erotic Bus Trip

The Blind Girl: An Erotic Romance(Coming Soon)

Lesbian Erotica Bundles:

Jade's Erotic Adventures: Books 1 - 5

Jade's Erotic Adventures: Books 6 - 10

Jade's Erotic Adventures: Books 11 - 15

Jade's Erotic Adventures: Books 16 - 20

Jade's Erotic Adventures: Books 21 - 25

Jade's Erotic Adventures: Books 26 - 30

Jade's Erotic Adventures: Books 31 - 35

Jade's Erotic Adventures: Books 36 - 40

Jade's Erotic Adventures: Books 41 - 45

Jade's Erotic Adventures: Books 46 - 50

Fifty Shades of Jade: Superbundle

Standalone Stories:

The Polynesian Girl: A Lesbian EroticRomance

For the uninhibited...

WANT TO AMP UP YOUR SEX LIFE?

Sign up for my newsletter to receive more free books and other steamy stuff. Discover a hundred different ways to wet your whistle!

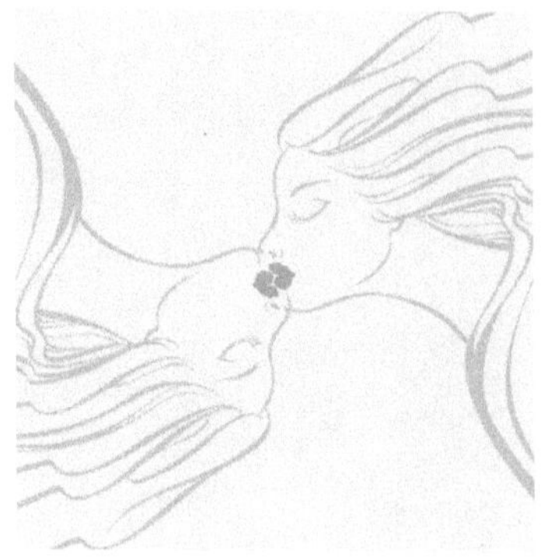

Victoria Rush Erotica

1

———

After their exciting adventure in the mermaid lagoon, Clover, Tara, and Jessop returned to the mainland, continuing their journey south along the coastline.

"This place just keeps getting better and better," Clover mused to her friends. "Erotic plants, friendly dragons, sexy mermaids, what other surprises does this magical land of Abbynthia have in store?"

"You never know until you round the next corner," Tara smiled, looking out over the glimmering sea.

"It's certainly a lot more interesting than *my* homeland," Jessop chuckled, adjusting his crotch as he reflected back on their last adventure. "I don't know how many strange creatures I can fuck before my dick begins to fall off."

"We can always send you back home if you don't think you're up for it," Tara said.

"Oh, I'm up for it, alright," Jessop smiled.

Clover glanced overhead, hearing some rumbling in the distance.

"It looks like we might have a storm coming in," she said. "We should try to find some shelter and settle in for the night."

"Look," Tara said, pointing toward a gap in the cliff next to the sea. "We can hole up there while we gather some provisions in the woods."

"Works for me," Clover nodded, peering at the cave. "It might not be as comfortable as the hammocks on the mermaid isle, but at least we'll be protected from the elements."

While Tara and Jessop disappeared into the woods to capture some wild rabbits for dinner, Clover prepared a fire near the entrance to the cave. After they skinned the rabbits and cooked them over the fire, they sat down under cover of the overhanging cliff, watching the heavy rain pelting the surface of the water.

Jessop peered up, noticing some large boulders perched precariously at the top of the cliff.

"Maybe we should go a little further inside the cave," he said. "Those things look like they could fall on us any second."

Tara glanced up and chuckled, shaking her head.

"They've probably been like that for centuries. You're being superstitious again. We've probably got a better chance of being struck by *lightning* than being buried by one of those."

"Maybe so," Jessop said, inching his body backwards on the sand. "But do you want to be the unlucky one who happens to be in the wrong place at the wrong time when they finally decide to pry loose?"

Clover's body shook when she heard a loud clap of thunder, then she glanced behind her into the cave.

"Jessop's probably right," she said, wanting to get out of the rain. "Why don't we see what's inside? That cave looks pretty deep. Maybe we'll find some *more* strange creatures to play with."

"You mean like a bear or a colony of bats?" Tara chuckled.

"Hmm," Clover said, beginning to have second thoughts. "Let's bring some burning logs with us to light the way. At least that way, we'll have a modicum of protection if we run into any trouble."

They each picked up a burning stump from the fire, then they followed Clover into the narrow passageway. The further they went, the darker and more constricted the cave became, until it seemed to reach a dead-end.

"Let's get out of here," Jessop said, peering up at the steep walls. "This place gives me the creeps."

"Wait," Clover said, noticing a dim light coming from a small gap on the upper ledge. "Where's that light coming from? I think someone else is here."

"Let's leave them to their business," Jessop said. "There can't be anything of interest this far underground. I'm starting to get claustrophobic."

"Come on, scaredy-cat," Clover said, peering up toward the ledge. "We said we wanted adventure when we decided to hook up. It should only take a minute..."

She braced her legs against the sides of the tunnel and began climbing up, then when she reached the top, she peered through the hole, bulging her eyes.

"What the–?" she said, shaking her head.

"What is it," Tara said.

"It's some kind of cavern," Clover said. "With torches lining the walls. It looks like somebody lives here."

"Does it appear safe?" Tara said. "Do you think we should continue?"

"I don't see any sign of danger," Clover nodded. "Come on, let's check it out."

Tara looked at Jessop, then she jumped up onto the wall, climbing her way up toward Clover.

Jessop sighed, shaking his head in resignation.

"Something tells me this is another one of your crazy ideas," he said, glancing at Tara's sexy ass while he followed her close behind.

When they squeezed through the narrow gap, they gasped, peering at the enormous cavern. Decorated with intricate erotic carvings on the walls, the room was ablaze in torchlight. In the center of the dome-shaped grotto was a large circular platform raised on wooden stilts, covered in straw and soft grass and surrounded by three tall chairs looking like lifeguard stations.

"What is *that*?" Jessop said, squinting at the strange-looking structure.

"It almost looks like some kind of bed," Tara nodded.

"But I don't see anyone around," Clover said, glancing around the cavern, noticing a small hole in the ceiling of the dome. "This place reminds me a bit of the Pantheon in Rome."

"More like the Khajuraho Temple in India," Tara said, studying the assortment of friezes showing animals and couples engaged in all manner of sexual depravity.

"Whoever lives here," Jessop nodded. "It would have taken them *centuries* to finish all those detailed sculptures. Either that, or they've got an army of kinky craftsmen to do their bidding."

"Let's take a closer look," Clover said, climbing down the embankment into the heart of the chamber.

While they walked slowly around the perimeter of the chamber studying the depictions of men, women, and animals engaged in various positions of carnal activity, they didn't notice three scantily clad women emerge from hidden holes in the walls, wearing strange costumes and spiked headdresses.

2

———

"Do you find our sculptures interesting?" one of the women said.

Clover swung around, peering at the three women advancing toward them, shaking her head apologetically.

"Sorry if we're invading your home," she said. "We were just taking refuge from the storm, and kind of stumbled upon this place."

"I'd hardly say you *stumbled* upon it," one of the other women said. "It's a bit of a winding path getting in here. This must have aroused more than your usual curiosity."

"It's certainly arousing *something*," Tara said, fascinated with the intricate detail of the sculptures. "Did you carve these frescoes?"

"We had a little help from some of our friends," the third woman said.

"Friends?" Jessop said. "Do more people live here?"

"I'd say they're more like our guests," the third woman smiled. "Would you like to meet them?"

Clover peered at her friends, then back in the direction of the strangely dressed women.

"Perhaps we should introduce ourselves first," she said, stepping toward the first woman and extending her hand. "My name's Clover, and these are my friends Tara and Jessop."

"My name's Lucinda," the woman said, clasping Clover's hand firmly. "And these are my sisters, Nissa and Petunia."

"Sisters?" Clover said, pinching her eyebrows together. "Do you live here together?"

"Yes."

"Don't you find it a little claustrophobic? What do you do for food and water, closed up in this confined space?"

"The gods bring us everything we need from outside," Lucinda said, peering up at the hole in the ceiling spraying down a torrent of rain collected by the apparatus in the center of the floor, channeling the water along handmade gutters into large stone cisterns.

Tara walked up to the second woman and extended her hand to introduce herself while she peered at her strange headdress.

"Where did you get those interesting hats?" she said, narrowing her eyes. "They almost look like they're made out of bones..."

"Yes," Petunia said. "You'd be surprised what kind of creatures make their way in here. Besides giving us sustenance, we find their skeletons quite beautiful."

"As are you," Jessop smiled, approaching the third woman while he ran his eyes over her revealing costume. She wore some kind of animal-hide outfit, cut away at the front and back to expose her deep cleavage and round buttocks.

"You're quite a specimen yourself," Nissa said, stroking

her finger over the side of Jessop's face and over his muscular shoulders.

Clover paused for a moment, examining the wooden platform with a wrinkled forehead.

"Do you only use this structure for collecting water?" she said, bending down to peer underneath it.

"No," Lucinda said, glancing at Clover's ass while she bent over. "It serves a variety of purposes. We like to think of it more as a stage for our periodic entertainment."

"Entertainment?" Clover said. "What kind of entertainment?"

"The most interesting kind, of course," Lucinda said, peering toward her sisters. "Would you like to view one of our performances?"

"Has this got something to do with the erotic sculptures on your walls?" Clover said.

"In a manner of speaking," Lucinda smiled.

Tara glanced at her friends to see what they thought of the idea, and Clover and Jessop shrugged. Maybe it was the erotic images of fornication plastered all over the walls or the sexy figures of the scantily clad hosts that was biasing their opinion, but they seemed in no hurry to leave. Seeing as how the sisters had no visible form of defense, whereas they still carried their bow, sword, and bullwhip, it seemed like a safe bet.

"Okay," she nodded.

"Make yourselves comfortable," Lucinda said, motioning toward the tall chairs. "We'll be back momentarily."

The women retreated through an opening in the sidewall and when they returned, they were followed by three naked men and women, walking behind them with vacant expressions on their faces. When they reached the platform, the women motioned for them to scale a wooden ladder to the top, then the women climbed up the back of the raised chairs, positioning themselves behind each of the friends.

"Who are these people?" Clover said to Lucinda while the woman wrapped her legs softly around Clover's hips from behind.

"Guests, like you," she said.

"Why are they naked?"

"It's part of the performance," Lucinda smiled, stroking the sides of Clover's shoulders.

"Why do they look dazed?"

"You'll find out soon enough," Lucinda said, tracing her hands slowly down the sides of Clover's back.

A few moments later, the nude performers divided into three pairs, one boy-girl pair, one girl-girl pair, and one boy-boy pair. While they slowly began to caress and grope one another, they lowered themselves onto the dripping grass, pulling their bodies closer together and beginning to writhe in pleasure. Clover could see the men's penises beginning to harden and the women's mouths gaping open in obvious pleasure while they joined together in carnal union.

As she began to squirm her hips in unconscious arousal watching the spectacle, Lucinda's hands circled around the front of her tunic, caressing the front of her crotch while she squeezed Clover's breasts with her other hand. Whatever strange scheme these sisters had cooked up in their underground playpen, Clover was soon pulled into the performance, finding herself increasingly turned on by the erotic show playing out on the stage and the expert ministrations of her host pressing her breasts into her back.

She glanced over at Jessop, who had his pants unbuttoned while Nissa stroked his erection from behind with two hands. He seemed transfixed with the action on the stage, all the more aroused by the sight of the falling rainfall moistening their bodies and making them glisten in the soft torchlight illuminating the cavern. Then she peered over at Tara, noticing her smock rolled down the front of her body while Petunia's hands slipped down the front, circling her fingers over Tara's undulating pussy. There was something incredibly exciting about being stimulated from behind that none of the trio could resist while they watched the erotic performance of the sexy strangers on the stage with the rain pouring down on them like some kind of Hollywood special effect.

"Are you enjoying the performance, Clover?" Lucinda whispered into her ear.

"Yes," Clover panted. "Though I'm not sure which I'm enjoying more, the sexy performers or your caresses of my body."

"Which pairing do you find most exciting?" Lucinda said, pressing her fingers harder against Clover's twitching clit while she circled them over her dripping vulva.

"They're all incredibly sexy," Clover nodded, darting her eyes between each of the couples.

The heterosexual couple were locked in an embrace with the girl on top of the prone man as she rocked her body back and forth over his tightening balls while she tilted her head upward, feeling the rainwater drip all over her face. The lesbian couple were facing one another in a bent-knee sitting position, grinding their pussies together while they kissed each other passionately. And the two gay men were kneeling in the grass, frotting each other as they wrapped their hands tightly around their joined erections, jerking their hips in unison while they groaned into each other's mouths.

As they increased the pace of their gyrations and the volume of their groans, Clover felt the pangs of pleasure beginning to spread in her pelvis, and when she saw the two men shooting thick ropes of cum over each of their bellies, her hips began to quiver while Lucinda slipped two of her fingers into her pussy, jilling her quickly to orgasm.

"Holy shit," she panted after she came down from a long and hard climax. "This is quite a circus you've created in this little hideaway. Who knew anyone could have so much fun in a hole in the ground?"

"I'm glad you liked it," Lucinda said, noticing her friends shaking in their own throes of climax from their elevated viewing positions. "Something tells me you three will be a welcome addition to our troupe."

3

———

"A ddition?" Clover said. "How do you mean?"

"You obviously enjoyed watching our performers having sex," Lucinda smiled. "Wouldn't you prefer to participate in it *directly*?"

"You mean having sex with them on the stage?"

"Yes."

"I don't know..." Clover said, still not sure what kind of operation the three women were running.

"Oh, come now, Clover," Lucinda said, stroking her wet pussy. "You're still dripping in excitement. Don't tell me you wouldn't like to fuck some of those pretty boys and girls?"

Clover peered down at the glistening bodies of the sexy performers, feeling her pussy twitching.

"How would that work exactly?" she said.

"You simply climb the ladder and take your pick of who you'd like to play with. You can choose a man or a woman or a group of them if you prefer."

"But they've never even *met* me," Clover said. "How would I know they'd be interested in having sex with me?"

"Oh, they'll be *interested*, alright," Lucinda nodded. "Just like your other two friends are."

Clover glanced in the direction of the other two chairs and noticed Tara and Jessop walking aswoon toward the platform. When they reached the top, Jessop took the hands of the lesbian pair while Tara joined the boy-girl duo.

"The early bird gets the worm," Lucinda grinned. "You better get up there before the other two boys decide to get started with someone else."

Clover glanced at the thick organs of the gay men rubbing their erections against their stomachs while they kissed each other, feeling her pussy throbbing imagining how much she could enjoy two dicks at the same time. She climbed down Lucinda's chair and scaled the ladder to the platform, pulling off the rest of her clothes and placing them on the side of the stage. When she approached the two men, they smiled and separated to allow Clover to press her body against them.

"Would you boys like to play with something softer?" she smiled.

When they nodded, she reached out to stroke their slippery cocks, still coated in semen. They moaned and Clover sunk to her knees, licking their balls as the rain water from the overhead oculus dripped down over their bellies and her face. She felt their testicles beginning to elevate in rising sexual excitement, then she lifted her face a few inches and wrapped her mouth around their two crowns, licking and stroking their bulbs while they humped her face slowly. She peered out of the corner of her eye, noticing Jessop lying on the wet grass with the two women facing one another on his belly while they rubbed their pussies together against his flapping cock, giving her an idea.

"Lie down, facing each other, balls to balls," she told the two men.

The men peered at one another, then lay down as she'd instructed, with their hard dicks twitching over their rippling stomachs. Clover took one look at the cock sandwich, then she kneeled over their hips, pulling their organs together and pointing their tips toward her slit. As she lowered herself over their pulsating poles, all three of them groaned. When the men's dicks were all the way inside her, she leaned forward, placing her hands over the hard pecs of the younger man, beginning to rock her hips up and down.

While she reveled in the feeling of two hard cocks inside her, she glanced in the direction of Tara's threesome, watching her sixty-nining the other girl while the boy fucked her from behind. As she grunted from the pounding action of the man behind her, she peered up, looking at Clover with a wild look in her eyes.

Can you believe this? she mouthed, her face beginning to flush from the combined sexual stimulation.

"I told you we might find something interesting in here," Clover smiled, rolling her eyes back in her head from the pleasurable sensation of two hot dicks inside her pussy.

Then she heard Jessop grunting from the other side of the platform, while he squeezed the tits of the woman with his back to him as the two lesbians slid their dripping pussies up and down his beet-red pole.

"I will never doubt you again," he grinned.

As she watched her friends enjoying their impromptu threesomes, she peered around the room at the twisted positions of the lovers carved into the walls. Depicting thousands of different positions and combinations, she began to realize just how limited her sexual experiences had been up to this point.

This must be some kind of sex temple, she thought. *If this is any indication of what lies ahead, I'm glad we stumbled upon this place.*

Then she peered up, noticing the three women sitting in their elevated chairs with their legs spread apart, stroking their pussies while they watched the activity below.

Or maybe it's just a kinky BDSM club, here for the amusement of these strange ladies.

Soon after, each of the groups on the platform to begin howling in pleasure, falling into a deep slumber after they climaxed together.

4

When Clover awoke, she found herself lying in a pile of hay, surrounded by a group of naked men and women peering at her with vacant expressions. She tilted her head, noticing that she was in some kind of cage with iron bars.

"Where am I?" she said, lifting herself up groggily.

"You're in the witches' dungeon," one of the girls she recognized from the platform said.

"Witches?" Clover said, pinching her eyebrows. "What kind of dungeon?"

"This is where they take us after they've had their way with us," one of the boys from Jessop's pairing said.

"I don't understand," Clover said, shaking her head. "Why can't I remember what happened to me?"

"They put some kind of spell on us," another girl said. "It stimulates our libido and forces us to submit to their demands."

Clover peered around the enclosure, recognizing some of the other people from the stage. But Jessop and Tara were nowhere to be found.

"Where did they put my friends?" she said, suddenly sitting up.

"They put them in the other holding cells," the first girl said, pointing to two adjacent enclosures.

Clover narrowed her eyes, noticing the familiar forms of Tara and Jessop lying motionless on the grass.

"Jessop, Tara!" she yelled, rushing to the front of the cage and shaking the bars. "Are you alright?"

The two friends stirred and peered up, looking at their unusual surroundings with surprise.

"Clover," Tara said, staggering to the front of her cage. "Where are we? Why are we behind bars?"

"Apparently this is some kind of sex prison," Clover said. "The other prisoners say those women are witches. They put a spell on us after we climaxed, then they brought us back here."

"A sex prison?" Jessop said, shaking his head as tottered toward the front of his cage. "I knew this was too good to be true. What have you gotten us into this time, Clover?"

"I didn't hear you complaining when those two women were sucking your dick," Clover grunted.

"That's before I knew they were going to lock us up afterwards."

"Alright," Tara said, peering around the prison compartment. "Let's keep our heads about us. We've gotten out of stickier jams than this before. Let's get all the facts before we begin to panic."

Clover turned around to peer at some of the other prisoners locked in her enclosure.

"How long have you been here?" she said. "And how did you find this place?"

"Some of us have been here for *months*," the cute girl from Tara's pairing said. "We came here the same way you did, through the secret passageway leading in from the beach."

"Has anyone ever escaped?" Tara said.

"Some of the inmates disappear from time to time," the girl said. "We have no idea where they go. But they're almost always older."

"Or fat," one of the other inmates said.

"Shut up, Chad," the girl said, pushing the boy and making him topple over into the hay. "You're no perfect specimen yourself, with your tiny little dick."

Another girl stepped forward, placing herself between the belligerent inmates.

"We suspect the witches cull the group from time to time, saving the youngest and sexiest ones for their own amusement," she nodded.

"*Cull* them?" Jessop said, rattling the door to his cage to see if he could loosen it. "What do they do with the ones they remove?"

"Like I said," the first girl said. "We have no idea. Maybe they let them go after they've decided they have no more use for them."

"That doesn't make any sense," Tara said, shaking her head. "They'd risk having the freed prisoners report the location of this place to the authorities."

"Maybe they just *kill* them," Jessop said, shaking the door loudly. "Did you notice their weird headdresses made out of bones?"

"We've never seen any graves or bone fragments scattered around the cavern," the pretty girl said. "Whatever they do with them, they seem to just disappear into thin air."

The three friends peered at one another, shaking their heads.

"Now I see why they wanted to get us out of our clothes,"

Jessop said. "Without our weapons, we have no way of getting out of here."

"There's only three of them and scores of us," Tara said, glancing at the naked figures of the other prisoners. "We know there's at least two ways out of here. We just need to bide our time until their backs are turned and we can make our escape."

"You haven't noticed the *gargoyles*?" the first girl said.

"The what?" Clover said, widening her eyes.

"There's three of them," the girl nodded. "The witches seem to keep them as pets. They guard the exits and bring food in from the hole in the roof."

"Great," Jessop groaned, remembering how the three friends had left their pet dragon behind on the island of Sappho. "Where's *Rex* when we need him now?"

5

A few hours later, the witches entered the prison compartment, leading three gargoyles by a chain around their necks. While Clover and her friends peered at the grotesque creatures with their horned heads, werewolf bodies, and huge bat-shaped wings, the rest of the prisoners retreated to the rear of their enclosures, cowering in fear.

"What do you *want* with us?" Clover said, stepping to the front of her cage.

Lucinda strolled up next to Clover, and the gargoyles growled, baring their fangs.

"Isn't it obvious?" she said. "We want to play with you."

"And watch you play with the others," Petunia grinned.

"Then why do you need to lock us up?" Tara said, standing just far enough behind the bars to avoid the gargoyles' razor-sharp claws.

"We're not finished with you yet," Nissa said, reaching through the bars to stroke Jessop's pendulant tool. "We wouldn't want you leaving before we explored all the possibilities."

"So, you'll let us leave if we cooperate with your twisted plan?" Tara scowled.

"You won't be locked up forever," Lucinda smiled. "We just want to test your limits first."

"Test our limits how?" Jessop said.

"We've already seen what you can do with two *women*," Nissa grinned, caressing Jessop's thickening appendage. "Now we want to see what you can do with a *different* type of creature."

"Creature?" Jessop said, pinching his eyebrows. "What kind of creature?"

"All will become apparent soon enough," Lucinda grinned, waving her hand at the three friends and opening their crates to lead them back in the direction of the cavern.

Clover felt groggy again, and as she and the others followed Lucinda with other witches trailing behind, she felt a strange tingling in her belly, feeling her nipples hardening the closer she got to the platform.

"Up you go," Lucinda said, stopping at the base of the ladder.

"All of us?" Tara said.

"Yes," Petunia nodded, pulling the snarling gargoyles closer to the trio to encourage them to climb the ladder.

"Who will we be having sex with?" Jessop said, looking up at the empty platform.

"We'll send someone to join you soon enough," Nissa grinned, petting the heads of her pets standing obediently beside her.

When the three friends got up to the raised platform, the witches positioned the gargoyles in equal spaces around the base of the circle, then they climbed onto their elevated chairs, placing their hands over the armrests.

"What do you want us to do now?" Clover said, peering at the witches with a confused expression.

Lucinda nodded toward the gargoyles, and they flapped their wings, rising up to the platform and sitting quietly in front of each friend.

"You want us to have *sex* with these hideous creatures?" Tara said, bulging her eyes.

"They're not *always* so hideous," Lucinda smiled. "If you show them a little tenderness, I think you'll find they can be quite receptive."

Clover looked into the eyes of her gargoyle, remembering how their pet dragon Rex had warmed up to her after she'd nursed him back to health from an injury. She reached out to stroke his pointed ears, and he began to purr, rubbing his butt on the soft grass of the platform. She glanced between his legs, noticing his flaccid penis beginning to press outward. At first, she was frightened by the size of his organ, but the more aroused he became, the more his scaly skin softened and morphed into the flesh-like skin of a human.

As she moved her hand down over his shoulder, the animal slowly metamorphosized into a handsome man with muscular pecs and powerful arms. She peered over at Tara and Jessop who were watching the scene with keen interest, and she nodded toward them, encouraging them to follow her lead. Already aroused by the witches' spell, they reached out to touch their gargoyles, stroking their bodies until they also morphed into two muscular men.

Before long, the three pairs melded together, kissing one another as they ran their hands over each other's naked bodies. While the three witches looked on from their elevated chairs, the couples sunk to their knees, groping their genitals with wild abandon. For a moment, Clover wondered why all of the gargoyles were male, but after her exciting experience with the two gay men previously, she was eager to feel another cock in her pussy.

Even Jessop seemed mesmerized by his male partner, sucking his enormous penis on his knees while he rubbed his pole up and down with two hands. She peered over at Tara, who was lying flat on her back while her partner kneeled between her legs, lifting her knees and positioning his throbbing organ over her slit. When he pushed it inside her, he grabbed the sides of her ass, pulling her body back and forth over the soft grass while the witches circled their clits from above.

Becoming more aroused watching the erotic scene unfold, Clover peered toward her partner, placing her hands around his neck and wrapping her legs around his hips while she lowered her pussy over his upturned dick. Positioning her ass in Lucinda's direction to give her the best view of their performance, she reached behind her and squeezed the man's balls, making him groan while he pounded her pussy on his knees.

If they want an erotic performance, then that's what we'll give them, Clover thought, feeling her pleasure beginning to mount as she angled her twitching clit along the top of the man's flexing penis. She peered over at Jessop and noticed him hunched over on his palms while his partner squatted behind, pounding his thick organ into his ass while he jack-hammered Jessop's hard-on with his free hand.

"That's it, my boys," Lucinda purred. "Fuck them hard to quench your lust. Are you enjoying the fresh meat?"

"Unggh," the three transformed gargoyles growled, approaching the peak of their pleasure.

"Come for me, boys," Lucinda panted, jilling her pussy hard while she leaned forward to ogle the sexy scene. "Let's show our new friends what it feels like to climax like a *real* animal."

Clover could feel her passion spreading over her hips, and as she glanced over at her two friends, she saw them quivering in ecstasy while their partners grabbed their asses, burying their huge dicks deep inside their bowels. Feeling her own partner tightening his grip on her ass, she squeezed his testicles harder, feeling herself passing over the point of no return. When she began spraying her juices over his balls, he dug his nails into her back, arching his body and howling like a wolf while he spurted his seed inside her.

Moments later, Clover began to feel groggy, fluttering her eyes as her partner pulled out of her, slowly beginning to transform back into the form of a gargoyle. Before she fell asleep, she turned her head to peer at her friends, who lay on the dripping grass with contented smiles on their faces while the gargoyles stood over them with thick ropes of cum dripping from the ends of their throbbing cocks.

6

———————

When she awoke a few hours later lying in the soft straw of her prison enclosure, Clover tilted her head, noticing the pretty girl from her first pairing peering back at her.

"Gargoyle sex?" the girl said with a knowing smile.

"Mmm," Clover nodded. "It wasn't as bad as I thought it would be."

"Not when they transform into those gorgeous hunks with dicks the size of a horse," the girl grinned.

"Yeah," Clover said, placing her hand over her aching pussy. "I don't know how often I'll be able to do that again."

"I don't think you'll need to," the girl said, noticing the three witches re-entering the chamber without their pets. "It looks like the witches have come to satisfy a *different* kind of desire this time."

Clover raised up on her arms, watching the witches unlocking the cells and motioning for two inmates to follow them back into the main chamber.

"You two," Lucinda said, pointing her finger toward the

small-dicked boy and an older woman. "It's finally your turn to be set free."

"You're *releasing* us?" Chad said, sitting up eagerly.

"In a manner of speaking," Lucinda nodded, holding his hand as he slipped through the partially opened door.

Clover watched them exiting their crates under the supervision of the other witches, then she rushed to the front of her enclosure. Something didn't feel right, and she glanced toward her two friends, shaking her head suspiciously.

"Where are you taking them?" she said to the witches.

"To a better place," Lucinda said, escorting them out of the chamber. "Somewhere you'll all end up, eventually. Somewhere quiet and peaceful, where they'll finally be free."

"A *better* place?" Jessop said, peering at Clover and Tara with a wrinkled forehead. "Does that mean they're letting them go?"

"I have no idea," Clover said, glancing toward the pretty girl standing next to her.

After the witches left the chamber, everyone rushed toward the front of their enclosures and turned their heads against the bars, trying to listen to what was happening on the other side of the cavern. Clover could hear some rustling noises, followed by the flapping of wings, then a warm draft entered the prison enclosure.

"Is that...*smoke*?" Tara said, twitching her nose at the familiar scent of burning wood.

Suddenly, the chamber was filled with the sound of blood-curdling screams while everyone peered at one another with a frightened expression.

"That doesn't sound like the sound of *pleasure*," Jessop said, shaking his head.

Shortly after, a pungent odor began to waft into the compartment as the prisoners scrunched their faces into disgusted scowls.

"Oh my God," Clover said, suddenly realizing why the witches had taken the prisoners. "I think they're burning them alive!"

"It must be some kind of sacrificial ceremony," Tara said.

Suddenly, the pretty girl standing next to Clover threaded her arm between Clover's, shivering in fright.

"Is this what's to become of the rest of us?" she said.

"Not for a while, I expect," Clover said, holding the girl's arm tightly. "You're young and pretty, so I don't imagine they'll be taking you anytime soon."

Then she glanced over in the direction of Tara and Jessop.

"We've got to find a way out of here," she said. "We don't know how much longer it will be before they come back to cull the rest of the group."

"How do you propose to do that?" Jessop said, shaking the bars of his cell violently. "Unless you know how to bend steel with your bare hands."

Clover paused for a moment, remembering some of the survival tricks her brothers had taught her back in Tennessee.

"Do you remember where the witches put your clothes after we had sex with the other prisoners on our first day?"

"No," Jessop said. "I just remember laying them on the side of the platform, then falling asleep afterwards. I didn't see them when we returned later this morning."

"They must have put them *somewhere,*" Clover said. "Especially your sword and Tara's bow and arrow. They must have put them in safekeeping to make sure we couldn't find them again."

"What were you thinking of doing with them?" Tara said, narrowing her eyes at Clover. "How can those weapons help us escape from a locked jail cell?"

"All we need is Jessop's leather belt and a strong lever," Clover said. "We might be able to fashion a device to bend steel after all."

"What about the gargoyles?" Jessop said. "Even if we were able to free ourselves from these cages, how would we ever get past them?"

"We know they have at least one weakness," Clover smiled. "If we can convince them we only want to have sex with them, maybe we can distract them long enough to let everybody escape."

"Aren't you forgetting about something?" Tara said. "What about the *witches*? They'll just put another spell on us to keep us from escaping."

"They have to sleep sometime," Clover said. "We just have to plan our escape when they're not looking."

7

———

The next day, the witches returned to the prison enclosure with the gargoyles by their side. The animals had returned to their ill-tempered state, growling at any inmate who ventured too close to the bars. But Clover recognized the one with a nick in its ear, and when she reached out her hand, it licked her softly.

"Isn't that sweet?" Lucinda said. "Trozan seems to like you."

Then she pulled on the chain around the gargoyle's neck, dragging him away from the bars.

"But you mustn't get too friendly with the prisoners," she said, peering into his eyes. "Remember your main duty here."

"Which is to keep them in line," Petunia said.

"And to provide entertainment for us," Nissa said, grinning toward Jessop with a sly smile.

"What else can you possibly want with us?" Tara said. "Haven't we already provided you with enough entertainment? We've done everything you've asked, including have sex with your animals."

"That's true," Lucinda said. "But there's still *one* group you haven't had sex with."

Nissa reached through the bars of Jessop's cage, grabbing hold of his penis and pulling him close to her.

"You?" Clover said, shaking her head. "I thought you only liked to *watch*?"

"Most of the time," Lucinda smiled. "But sometimes, like our oversexed pets here, we like to participate in the action directly."

"And after your performance yesterday," Petunia said, staring at Tara's naked elf figure. "We think you three are just the ones to satisfy our curiosity."

Clover paused for a moment, peering at the three witches.

"If we do this, will you give us back our clothes?"

"I can't imagine what you'd need them for," Lucinda said. "It's not like you'll be socializing with outsiders anytime soon."

"It can get chilly in here at night," Clover said. "And the straw is prickly on our naked bodies. It would be far more comfortable to have something covering us while we sleep."

"I suppose it can be arranged," Lucinda said, nodding toward the other witches. "Of course, we'll have to keep your weapons in safekeeping."

"Of course," Clover nodded.

"Well then," Lucinda said, unlocking the cells while the gargoyles stood watch. "Shall we get this party started?"

The witches escorted the three friends out of their cells then marched them toward the main cavern. When they neared the platform, Clover noticed some ash and charred logs under the newly constructed stage.

It looks like they use these gargoyles for more than just protection and amusement, she thought, peering at the overhead oculus. The hole seemed just large enough to allow the animals to fly through it and supply the witches with whatever food and other provisions they needed.

"You boys stay here and make sure our pretty friends don't get any ideas about leaving," Lucinda said, positioning the gargoyles in a triangular pattern around the circular stage.

"You know the drill," Nissa said, motioning for the trio to climb the ladder.

"Are you going to join us?" Jessop said, smiling at the pretty witch.

"After you," she nodded, staring at Jessop's swinging dick as he scaled the ladder after Clover and Tara.

When they got to the top, Clover peered at Jessop with an angry expression.

"Don't get too friendly with these witches," she said, furrowing her brows. "Don't forget what they did with the other prisoners."

"We might as well enjoy ourselves while we're stuck in this place," he shrugged.

"You're disgusting," Tara grunted, glaring at the witches as they climbed atop the platform.

"It looks like we'll have to put our guests in the proper mood," Petunia said, waving her hand toward Tara, making her go limp and tingly.

"It's too bad," Lucinda said, pulling off her clothes and waving her hand as she approached Clover. "I would have liked to see what they're capable of when they have all of their wits about them."

"This one doesn't seem to need any extra encouragement," Nissa said, peering at Jessop's rising erection.

"Let's see if they're as good at satisfying a *woman* as a

man," Petunia said, pressing her body against Tara and kissing her softly while she caressed her pointy ears.

Clover felt tingly again, and she peered at Lucinda's naked figure as the witch moved in closer. She had the soft skin of a much younger woman, with plump breasts and curvy hips framing a strawberry-colored patch of pubic hair over her toned abdomen. Unable to resist the witch's charms, they pressed their bodies together, lowering them-selves to the surface while they caressed each other's bodies.

Lucinda pressed Clover down onto the grass, then she straddled one of her legs, grabbing her toes and thrusting them inside her dripping pussy. As she raised and lowered her hips, thrusting Clover's foot deeper and deeper into her hole, she peered at Clover with a glazed expression, groaning while her juices leaked out of her slit and down Clover's foot.

As much as Clover resented the witches holding them in captivity and subjecting them to their depraved schemes, there was something about their beautiful figures and beguiling faces that Clover found irresistible. As she watched Lucinda fucking her foot, she slid her fingers over her mound, slipping them inside her slit and curling them next to her G-spot, feeling her pleasure beginning to mount.

When she heard Jessop groaning nearby, she turned her head, noticing Nissa hunched over his hard-on in the reverse cowgirl position, bending over to suck his toes. Judging by the expression on Jessop's face, he seemed to enjoy the stimulation as much as his partner, digging his fingers into the sides of Nissa's ass while she moaned in delight.

Then she swung her head in Tara's direction, watching Petunia holding her elevated leg between her breasts while she kneeled between Tara's thighs, rubbing their pussies together as she licked the bottom of Tara's foot.

So that's their thing, Clover nodded, watching the three witches grunting while they played with their partners' feet. *Who would have thought it would be a foot fetish?*

Before long, all three witches were moaning and convulsing in orgasmic pleasure while they sucked, tribbed, and caressed their partner's feet. The three friends seemed equally turned on by the experience, climaxing soon after, with everybody collapsing in a panting heap next to one another. Even the gargoyles seemed excited by the erotic performance, jerking their giant erections until they sprayed their jism in three tall arcs toward the stage.

8

———————

After the witches recovered from their orgasms and climbed down from the platform, Lucinda gathered their clothes and escorted the three friends back to the prison enclosure under the watchful eye of the gargoyles. Before entering her cell, Clover noticed a broken log lying in the dirt, and she kicked it toward the side of the cage while Lucinda was locking up the others.

"You three are a lot of fun," she smiled, tossing their togs inside the enclosures after she locked the doors. "But don't get too comfortable in those clothes, we'll be wanting you naked again soon enough."

After Lucinda returned to the main cavern, Clover waited a few minutes, then she peered at the broken log lying in the sand. She couldn't reach it with her arm, but after wedging her legs between the bars, she was able to slide it close enough to pull it into the cage.

"Now what?" Jessop said, watching from the other cell. "Do you think you can bend these bars with a piece of wood?"

"Not *only* with a piece of wood," Clover smiled, peering at Jessop's pants. "Throw me your belt."

"Fine," Jessop said, unbuckling his belt and tossing it through the gap. "But I don't see how that's going to be any help."

Clover wrapped the belt around two adjacent bars in her cage, then she threaded the log between the strap, beginning to twist it slowly. As the belt began to tighten around the bars, she grunted, trying to turn the handle further.

"Can you help me with this?" she said, glancing at one of the taller men in the cage.

"Sure," the man said, stepping toward the front of the enclosure. "What do you want me to do?"

"Hold one end of the stump and turn in clockwise while I turn the other end. We just need to create enough force to pull the strap tighter."

The man nodded at Clover, then he grabbed the stick, grunting as the two of them cranked it a few degrees clockwise. The bars started to creak, and Clover noticed them bending slowly toward one another.

"Holy shit!" Jessop said. "It's working! It's actually bending the bars!"

"Shh!" Clover said, letting go of the lever. "Do you want to let the witches know what we're doing?"

"Why are you stopping?" Jessop whispered.

"The steel makes too much noise when it bends," Clover said. "We're going to have to wait until the witches go to sleep before we go any further."

While the prisoners waited for the light to fade in the main cavern, Clover and others quietly plotted their escape. After they separated the bars enough to slip through the cage, Clover, Tara, and Jessop would make sure the witches were asleep, then they'd attempt to distract the gargoyles while the others slipped out the small entrance hole. If all went well, the three friends would be able to follow them out soon after, making their getaway before the witches realized what was happening.

When the light from the oculus grew dark and the cavern became quiet, Jessop turned toward Clover, eager to execute their plan.

"What are we waiting for?" he said. "Let's get the hell out of here!"

"Cool your jets," Clover said. "We're only going to have one chance at this. We need to make sure the witches are asleep first. Let's wait a few more hours before we make our move."

The time passed slowly, but when everything became still in the cavern, Clover nodded to the tall inmate and they resumed their cranking of the improvised tourniquet, slowly bending the bars together. But the gap still wasn't wide enough to fit a person through, so Clover moved the belt to the adjacent two bars, where she repeated the procedure. By the time they were finished, the four bars had been bent into two diamond shapes, with the gap between them just wide enough for Clover to slip through.

When she squeezed out of her cage, she tiptoed over to Tara and Jessop's cell, handing them the equipment and watching them bend the bars in a similar fashion. After everybody squeezed out of their enclosure, Clover instructed the group to pause at the entrance to the cavern while she ducked her head around the corner, looking for any sign of the witches. When she couldn't see them anywhere, she nodded toward her friends.

"It looks like they've gone into their holes for the night," she whispered. "But I can see the gargoyles sleeping on top of the platform. It will be too risky for us all to go out at the same time. The three of us will have to distract the gargoyles while the rest of you sneak out the exit."

"Distract them how?" Jessop said.

"It looks like the only safe way to pacify them is to have *sex* with them," Clover nodded.

"What happens when they're finished and they revert to their gargoyle shape?" Tara said. "How do we keep them from gobbling us up after they notice all the prisoners have escaped?"

Clover paused for a moment, remembering how the gargoyles had mutated when they had sex with them earlier.

"They seem to morph into humans when they're aroused, then transform back into their animal form after they climax," she nodded. "We just need to keep them aroused long enough for everybody to get out, then we can follow soon after."

"What if the witches wake up and try to come after us?" Jessop said. "The gargoyles look large enough for them to fly on their backs and put us back under a spell."

"We'll address that problem once we get out of here," Clover said. "Just try not to wake them up."

9

───────

Clover motioned for the other prisoners to wait a few minutes, then the three friends crept toward the platform, watching the gargoyles sleeping quietly on their backs. They climbed the ladder and as Clover approached Trozan, he stirred, snarling in her direction. She held out her hand, and when his ears pulled back, she kneeled between his legs, caressing his organ as it pushed out of its sheath.

Slowly he began morphing back into his human form, and when his tool reached its full length, Clover glanced over at her friends, who were kneeling in front of the other gargoyles, stroking them in a similar fashion. While the newly transformed men became increasingly distracted by their partners' attention, the rest of the group crept out from the prison enclosure, tiptoeing toward the exit.

That's it, Clover nodded, motioning for the prisoners to move quickly, behind Trozan's back. *We just need to keep them busy for a little longer...*

Suddenly, Trozan noticed some movement out of the corner of his eye, and he flinched, turning toward the prisoners. He growled, and Clover grabbed his chin, turning his face toward her.

"Trozan," she said, peering into his eyes. "Why don't you come with us? You're as much a slave to the witches as we are. Let us go, and we can all be free."

He peered at Clover with a confused expression, then she slid her hand over his dripping cock.

"Maybe we can find a way to remove this spell and return you to your human form *permanently*," she said. "Come with us and see what you've been missing on the outside."

He glanced toward the other gargoyles who had also noticed the fleeing prisoners, then he nodded silently. Seeing that the other gargoyles seemed to understand, Tara and Jessop stood up, taking them by the hand and leading them down the ladder. Knowing the best way to keep Trozan pacified was to keep him aroused, Clover grabbed his throbbing pole and escorted him off the platform, trying her best to keep him stimulated.

When the last of the prisoners had squeezed through the exit hole, Tara and Jessop nodded, following quickly after them. By now, the other two gargoyles had begun to transform back into their animal form, and they struggled to get through hole as their arms began spreading into wings. While they squawked and groaned trying to gain their freedom, suddenly the three witches appeared from the holes in the opposite wall, yelling for them to stop.

"Trozan!" Lucinda yelled, seeing Clover and the last gargoyle standing by the exit. "Stop her! Don't let her escape!"

Trozan peered at Clover with a frightened look, then he motioned for her to follow her friends through the hole.

"Go," he said in a half-animal voice. "I will protect you."

"What about *you*?" Clover said, seeing him beginning to morph back into his gargoyle form. "I can't leave you here alone."

"I'll come after you," Trozan nodded. "Go now!"

Lucinda waved her hand in their direction and Trozan stepped in front of Clover to block the spell, falling to his knees and going limp. Clover glared at the witch, then she ducked through the hole, chasing after the others toward the opening on the beach.

When everybody had escaped from the cave, they huddled together on the shore, unsure what to do next.

"What happened to Trozan?" Tara said, peering back in the direction of the passageway.

"He didn't make it," Clover said. "The witches transformed him just before I escaped."

"We better get out of here," Jessop said, peering at the two half-animal creatures standing next to them. "Who knows what these two will do when they revert back to their full animal form."

"Wait," Tara said, grabbing his hand. "The witches can still follow us. Shouldn't we try to block the cave or something?"

Clover peered up at the large boulders dangling at the top of the cliff, then she turned toward the gargoyles.

"Can you help us?" she said. "Can you fly up there and push those rocks over the cliff?"

They peered at Clover and the others for a moment, then they glanced at one another, nodding their heads. By now, their cocks had retraced fully back into their sheaths, and their bodies had returned to their natural gargoyle state. But they seemed to understand Clover's instructions, and when they flew to the top of the cliff, she motioned for everybody to step to the side. After the group moved back, they saw the boulders teetering, then there was a loud crash as they tumbled down the hillside, landing in a pile of dust, blocking the cave entrance.

When the gargoyles flew down to join the rest of the group, Tara threw her arms around them.

"Thank you for helping us," she said, petting their stomachs.

"What about the *other* hole?" Jessop said, shaking his head. "There's still one more gargoyle inside, and he could fly the witches to safety through the oculus. Shouldn't we close that one too?"

Clover glanced toward Tara, and she tilted her head, knowing Jessop was right. It would be far too dangerous to leave the witches any escape route, especially with one remaining gargoyle having the strength to clear away the boulders.

She peered at the two gargoyles, hoping they still could understand her.

"Can you fly us up to the roof?" she said.

They glanced at one another and nodded, and the three friends climbed onto their backs while the animals flapped their way to the top of the cliff. A few meters inland, they found the oculus, surrounded by a pile of boulders. Clover stepped to the edge and peered downward, noticing Trozan lying peacefully next to the three witches.

"Good," Jessop said, looking down the hole next to her. "Now's the perfect time to seal the lid, while the other gargoyle is sleeping."

When the witches heard the commotion from above,

they looked up, recognizing the three friends. They tried waving their hands in their direction, but this time, the spell didn't work.

"It looks like their powers are limited to the area inside the cavern," Clover nodded.

A few seconds later, Trozan began to stir, and the witches became excited, motioning for him to attack the fugitives.

"Trozan," Lucinda said, pointing upwards. "Capture the escapers!"

"Hurry," Jessop said, stepping back from the edge and motioning to the other gargoyles. "We've got to block the hole before he recovers his strength."

Clover hesitated, peering down into the cavern while Trozan gazed up at her.

"It's okay, Trozan," she called down. "We're your friends. Come with us, and we'll free you from the witches' evil spell."

Trozan tilted his head like a curious dog, then Lucinda slapped him hard across the face.

"Don't listen to her," she said. "You know who your masters are. *Kill her!*"

"What are we waiting for?" Jessop said, becoming increasingly impatient. "We've got to close the hole now!"

"Hold on," Clover said, peering at the other gargoyles. "The other ones seem to have shaken the witches' spell now that they're out of the cave. Maybe the same will happen with Trozan."

"*Maybe?*" Jessop said, shaking his head. "Do you really want to take the chance?"

Clover glanced back down into the hole, noticing Trozan's tail wagging while he looked up at her.

"Come on, baby," she called. "Leave those witches where they belong. Come join us and be free."

Trozan glanced up at Clover, then he tilted his head at the three witches.

"Don't even think about it," Lucinda glared, raising her hand to strike him again.

He pulled back his lips and snarled at her with his razor-sharp teeth, then he spread his wings, flapping up to the opening in the roof. When he flew out of the hole, he lowered himself beside Clover, licking her hand and panting softly.

"Good boy," Clover said, petting his head. "Now, let's close this hole so we never have to worry about these witches again."

While the other two gargoyles began rolling a giant rock toward the hole, Trozan joined his mates, raising it over the precipice.

When the witches realized they were about to be trapped inside, they screamed toward Clover.

"You can't trap us inside the cave!" Lucinda pleaded. "We'll die in here without food and water!"

"You should have thought of that when you were sacrificing the other inmates," Clover grinned. "At least this way, you'll die slower and less painfully."

Clover nodded toward the gargoyles holding the rock, and they tipped it over, sealing the hole with a loud thud.

"Now what?" Jessop said, glancing toward the three oversize gargoyles.

"It'll be getting light soon," Clover said, peering toward the orange glow on the horizon. "The prisoners will be hungry. We can hunker down on the beach for a while until we figure out our next move."

Then she peered at Trozan panting next to her, with his thick gargoyle cock slipping out of its sheath.

"Besides," she grinned. "I think we owe our new friends a little gratitude for helping us escape."

***

*R*eady for more erotic chills and thrills? Order the next exciting volume in Clover's Fantasy Adventures, *Rapunzel*. Buy direct and save at victoriarusherotica. Or download from your favorite online bookstore here: retailer links.

Not every girl wants to marry a prince...

ALSO BY VICTORIA RUSH

Adult Fairytales:

The Enchanted Forest: An Erotic Fairytale

The Land of Giants: An Erotic Fairytale

The Dragon's Lair: An Erotic Fairytale

Witch's Brew: An Erotic Fairytale

The Mage's Spell: An Erotic Fairytale

The Mermaid Lagoon: An Erotic Fairytale

The Coven: An Erotic Fairytale

Rapunzel: An Erotic Fairytale

The Seven Dwarfs: An Erotic Fairytale

The Land of Mutants: An Erotic Fairytale

The Erotic Temple: A Sexy Fairytale (Coming Soon)

Erotica Themed Bundles:

Voyeur: Lesbian Erotica Bundle

Public Affairs: A Lesbian Anthology

Futa Fantasies: The Ladyboy Collection

Threesomes: The Lesbian Collection

Threesomes - Volume 2: The Lesbian Collection

First Time: A Lesbian Anthology

Hedonism: An Erotic Anthology

Switch Hitters: Bisexual Erotica

Taboo Erotica: The Lesbian Series

BDSM: The Lesbian Collection

Party Games: The Erotic Collection

Party Games 2: The Erotic Collection

All Girl 1: Lesbian Erotica Bundle

All Girl 2: Lesbian Erotica Bundle

All Girl 3: Lesbian Erotica Bundle

All Girl 4: Lesbian Erotica Bundle

Erotic Fairytale Bundles:

Clover's Fantasy Adventures: Books 1 - 5

Clover's Fantasy Adventures: Books 6 - 10

Erotic Fantasy:

Pirate's Bounty: A Time Travel Adventure

Wild West: A Time Travel Adventure

Private Riley: A Time Travel Adventure

Cleopatra's Secret: A Time Travel Adventure

Bounty Hunter 2125: A Time Travel Adventure

Ninja Assassin: A Time Travel Adventure

The 300: A Time Travel Adventure

Arabian Nights: An Erotic Fairytale (coming soon...)

Steamy Time Travel Bundles:

Riley's Time Travel Adventures: Books 1 - 5

Lesbian Erotica:

The Dinner Party: Lesbian Voyeur Erotica

The Darkroom: Bisexual Voyeur Erotica

Naked Yoga: Lesbian Transgender Erotica

Nude Cruise: Bisexual Voyeur Erotica

Rush Hour: Taboo Public Sex

The Girl Next Door: First Time Lesbian Erotic Romance

Girls' Camp: Lesbian Group Sex

Wet Dream: Ladyboy Fantasy Erotica

The Convent: Taboo Sex with a Nun

Sex Robot: A Dream Sex Machine

The Personal Trainer: Getting Pumped at the Gym

The Dominatrix: BDSM Lesbian Domination

Webcam Chat: Lesbian Online Sex

Paint Me: A Kinky Bodypainting Workshop

The Toy Party: Girls Sharing Sex Toys

The Costume Party: Strapping One On

Swedish Sauna: Lesbian Group Sex

The Therapist: Taboo Lesbian Erotica

Elevator Shaft: Bisexual Threesomes Erotica

Ladyboy: Lesbian Transgender Erotica

Peep Show: Lesbian Voyeur Erotica

The Dare: Public Sex Erotica

Maid Service: Lesbian Threesomes Erotica

The Hitchhiker: First Time Lesbian Erotica

The Housesitter: Spycam Lesbian Erotica

The Spa: Lesbian Group Orgy

Parlor Games: Blindfold Sex Party

The Exchange Student: First Time Lesbian Erotica

The Hostel: Bisexual Group Erotica

The Harem: Lesbian Erotic Romance

The Orient Express: Lesbian Voyeur Erotica

The First Lady: A Forbidden Lesbian Erotic Romance

The Slave: Lesbian BDSM Erotica

The Masseuse: Lesbian Sensuous Erotica

Too Close for Comfort: Lesbian Forbidden Erotica

Naked Twister: A Wild Party Game

Lexi: The Sex App (Lesbian Fantasy Erotica)

Call Girl: Lesbian Bisexual Threesomes Erotica

Circle Jill: Lesbian Masturbation Workshop

The Viewing Room: Masturbation Voyeur Erotica

Spin the Bottle: A Kinky Party Game

The Hair Salon: Lesbian Voyeur Erotica

Tribadism 1: Girls Only Sex Workshop

Tribadism 2: The Art of Scissoring

Tribadism 3: Threeway Hookups

The Kiss: A Game of Oral Sex

Pledge Week: Sorority Sisters

Carny Games 1: A Wild Sex Party

Carny Games 2: A Kinky Sex Party

Carny Games 3: An Erotic Sex Party

Dreamscape: An Artificial Reality Game

Glory Hole: Guess Who's On the Other Side

Joy Ride: A Late Night Erotic Bus Trip

The Blind Girl: An Erotic Romance(Coming Soon)

Lesbian Erotica Bundles:

Jade's Erotic Adventures: Books 1 - 5

Jade's Erotic Adventures: Books 6 - 10

Jade's Erotic Adventures: Books 11 - 15

Jade's Erotic Adventures: Books 16 - 20

Jade's Erotic Adventures: Books 21 - 25

Jade's Erotic Adventures: Books 26 - 30

Jade's Erotic Adventures: Books 31 - 35

Jade's Erotic Adventures: Books 36 - 40

Jade's Erotic Adventures: Books 41 - 45

Jade's Erotic Adventures: Books 46 - 50

Fifty Shades of Jade: Superbundle

Standalone Stories:

The Polynesian Girl: A Lesbian EroticRomance

FOLLOW VICTORIA RUSH:

Want to keep informed of my latest erotic book releases? Sign up for my newsletter and receive a FREE bonus book:

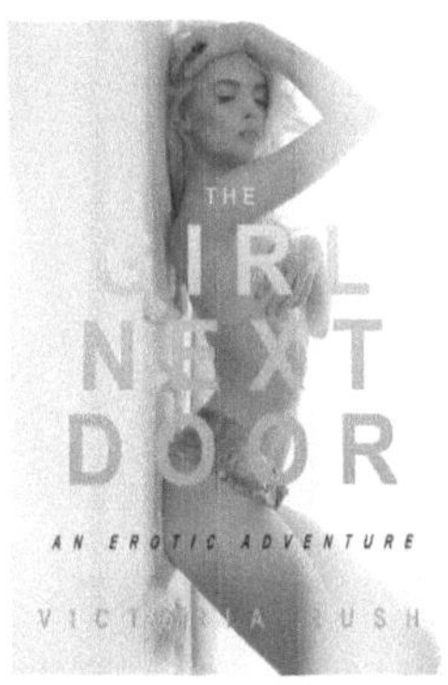

Spying on the neighbors just got a lot more interesting...

www.ingramcontent.com/pod-product-compliance
Lightning Source LLC
Chambersburg PA
CBHW061552310726
48972CB00008B/2723